SECOND WIFE

SECOND WIFE

stories

Winner of The Florida Review's Jeanne Leiby Award

RITA CIRESI

BURROW PRESS | ORLANDO, FL

Published by Burrow Press, in partnership with
The Florida Review's Jeanne Leiby Award.

Jeanne Leiby Award Series Editor: Susan Fallows
The Florida Review Editor: Lisa Roney
Cover & Book Design: Ryan Rivas

ISBN: 978-1-941681-89-3

Burrow Press
PO Box 533709
Orlando, FL 32853
burrowpress.com

This publication is made possible in part by our Founding Sponsors

ROLLINS

MASTER OF
LIBERAL STUDIES

Burrow Press thrives on the direct support of its subscribers, and generous support from grants, companies, foundations, and individuals.

Jeanne Leiby Award

In Memory of Jeanne Leiby, 1964–2011

As editor of *The Florida Review* from 2004 to 2007, Jeanne breathed new life into the University of Central Florida's literary journal. She brought graphic narratives to *TFR*, initiated the journal's first web site, published the special 30th anniversary issue, and brought together a smart team of graduate students and taught them to be editors.

Established after Jeanne's death in 2011, the award commemorates her commitment to writing and publishing by offering the winner both a monetary award and publication in the form of a chapbook.

Special thanks to this year's judge, Robert Venditti.

Patrons of the Jeanne Leiby Award

Pat and Jim Leiby
Bennet Heart and Anne Leiby
Rob Raff
Anonymous

CONTENTS

Bag Boy

My husband loves old-fashioned meatloaf: two parts beef to one part pork, three eggs, a cup of breadcrumbs, a dash of half and half, and a blanket of bacon and ketchup on top.

Back home—in Pennsylvania—the recipe is called Mom's Love.

Here in south Florida, it's so blasting hot I could fry bacon on our swimming-pool deck. Yet I still decide to make Mom's Love, because I miss home and the way its name sounds like a train that'll never stop: *Lackawanna, Lackawanna, Lackawanna.*

The grocery store unnerves me. All those moms pushing those looks-like-a-car momcarts. All those grandmothers in hairnets offering sample slices of Virginia ham and blocks of orange cheese on top of Triscuits.

I rush through the aisles. I've unloaded onto the belt all the meatloaf fixings—and the frozen peas, the Blue Bell ice cream, the Marie Callender's Dutch Apple pie—when I see him standing there at the end of the line, his butternut-squash-colored hair glinting in the fluorescent lights.

JEREMY, his nametag says.

I have seen JEREMY the bag boy before, messing around down the street on his skateboard, riding his mountain bike into the parking lot of our community rec center. He plays basketball—with half a dozen sweaty, shirtless boys in shorts—on the hot asphalt court, while inside the clubhouse, I try to work off that last five pounds on the elliptical.

Douche bag, the boys call each other, as they jostle at the outdoor water fountain. *Mama's boy. Faggot.*

Yesterday JEREMY was the last to take a drink. As he bent over the fountain, I stared—too hard—at the poke of his collarbone. The jut of his shoulder blades. The knuckles of his spine continuing down to the frayed elastic of his shorts.

The obvious-mom on the treadmill next to me clicked her tongue.

He could be your son, she said.

Yes, I wanted to say. *But he isn't.*

•

Cooking something good? JEREMY asks as he slides my eggs into a plastic bag.

Meatloaf, I tell him.

Can I come over for dinner?

The cashier—old enough, like me, to be called *ma'am*—frowns. But I smile and tell JEREMY *I would love that* when he asks if he can help me out to my car.

JEREMY pushes my cart the same way he rides his mountain bike: one hand only.

Hot out here, I say.

You just move here?

How'd you know?

Guessed, I guess. Where from?

Pennsylvania.

It snow a lot there?

Sometimes.

I've never seen snow.

I pop the trunk of my Toyota. As JEREMY unloads the bags, I keep my hands in my pockets—to keep myself from touching his hair, which looks warm as a pumpkin under the sun.

I've seen you before, I say.

Here?

I live down the street from you.

What grade your kids in?

I don't have kids.

Oh. JEREMY blinks, with the blue eyes that have never seen snow. That must be why I don't know you.

He holds up the last bag. Where do you want your eggs?

What?

Your eggs. They told us in training. Most ladies want the stuff that'll break up front.

JEREMY places the eggs on the passenger seat. For a second I get the weird feeling he's going to strap them in with the seatbelt. Then he straightens up.

Haveanicedayma'am!

In my rearview mirror, I see JEREMY get a running start, then mount the cart and ride it up the hot black asphalt to the front of the store.

Wheeee, I imagine him thinking.

But then I remember he is fifteen, sixteen, maybe seventeen years old. Which means he is thinking, *I wish this cart was a girl I could—*

•

Onto the black granite counter I unload the softened ice cream, warm milk, sweaty meat. The fleshy worms of the pale pork make my insides clutch up like those charts in the doctor's office that show the tangle of the ileum and duodenum and all the rest of the digestive tract.

I crack the eggs. Beat them with the cream. Crumble the bread. Squish together the chilled meat and ketchup and slop of eggs until my fingers grow so stiff I have to thaw them under hot water. I punch down the meat in the loaf pan and lay the bacon on top.

350 degrees. For one hour. The hour when Paul will come back from work and crank the AC so hard the sliding-glass doors will fog within seconds. He'll give me a kiss. Then give me that smile that causes everyone—including me—to call him a *great guy*.

Smells like home, he'll say, then peer through the grease-spattered window of the stove. Whatja got in the oven?

What will he do if I say Mom's Love?

Will he open the freezer, releasing a cloud of frosty white air, and crack a tray of ice cubes into the stainless steel sink with a fearsome clatter?

Will he ask me, Drink?

Or will he not-say: Don't you think we should talk about—?

I push back the sliding-glass door. Outside, I lie on the hot webs of the lounge chair and look at the sky. In the west the clouds are a sick sea green, like the algae crusting around the edge of the swimming pool because Paul still hasn't figured out how to clean it. But overhead the sky is the cheerful bright blue of the Rubbermaid water bottle I carry to the clubhouse every afternoon. Blue as the bumpers on JEREMY's basketball posts. Blue as the light that explodes behind my eyes when I hold Paul's body so tight against mine it seems inconceivable I could ever let him go.

Blue, but not as wrinkled, as the doctor's robe.

No more ice, the doctor told Paul, who'd been feeding me slivers for the past fifteen hours.

To me—his voice full of piss at being stuck in the delivery room in the middle of a blizzard—he said, Push.

I—am—pushing.

Harder.

Come on, Mary, Paul said. Give it all you've got.

•

I had given it all I had. The icicles in the window glittered and the clock read 7:16 at the moment when the doctor was supposed to hold up the goods and tell us, Say hello to your son. But outside snow kept falling like cotton and the delivery room went blank as wall-to-wall carpet.

Blue babies, they call them. But ours was gray, mottled as a fig, and felt heavy as a sack of cornmeal when they swaddled him in a white cotton receiving blanket and put him in my arms to say goodbye. I tried to memorize the snub of his nose, the width of his cheeks, the thatch of butternut-squash-colored hair. I wiped the mucus off his closed eyes, then put my finger between my lips and sucked his sad saltiness deep into my mouth.

Why, I don't know. But somehow I got it into my head I could take him home, in one of those square, silver bags hanging in the grocery store that read
KEEP HOT FOOD HOT
FROZEN FOOD FROZEN
I imagined myself unthawing him on the kitchen counter.

So when the nurse bent down to take him away, I held on tighter.

•

There was a scene.

In the end, I handed him off to Paul, who kissed his forehead and said, Goodbye, little boy.

Or maybe I just imagined Paul saying that. I couldn't hear squat, because my ears throbbed with sorrow and—knowing Paul and I had just become the couple who made other couples shake their head and say, *What a shame, why didn't they go to China?*—I was sobbing enough tears to fill a wok.

Precipitation: 50 Percent

Sitting in the oncologist's waiting room is like watching the weather report. While the Storm Team Meteorologist gasses on about wind speed, humidity, visibility, and dew point, I want to reach into the TV, grab this guy's necktie, and command him: *just tell me how hard it's going to rain.*

Second Wife

He hides the DVD in his study closet, at the bottom of a box marked ALLIED VAN LINES. But it's not his porn. It's mine.

I wait until two inches of snow coat the ground, so I'll hear his Infiniti crunch up the driveway if and when he comes home tonight. Only then do I slip the DVD into my laptop, which swallows it with a sick *suck*.

My heart does double-time.

I've watched this video so many times I have it memorized. The audible breath of the videographer. The swell of the organ. The plane of her bare shoulders, the pulse of her collarbone, the jut of her breasts in the sleeveless dress. The cocky way he steps forward to claim her.

There is nothing more obscene than watching your own husband marry his first wife, vowing to love and cherish, et cetera, until death, et cetera, in a confident voice that says nothing will ever break them apart.

But with *me*. With me. His voice broke in two when he said *I do*, as if he already heard in the distance the snow softly falling and the ice cracking along the eaves.

Depression, origin of

All the other Girl Scouts got happy when they ate their s'mores, but I just felt sorry for the marshmallow.

Physical Therapy

The therapist is half my age, but twice my size. He stands so close I can make out the threads on his polo shirt, so close he surely can whiff the liquid soap called Sensual I used that morning in the shower.

On a scale of 1 through 10, he asks, how bad is your pain today?

9, I lie. Because it feels so good the way he commands me to lie down on the vinyl bed. Stretches my legs. Lifts my hips. Pushes my knees into my chest. Tells me to push back. Harder. *Harder.*

At the end of the hour I put the forty-dollar co-pay on my husband's credit card. And as I walk out of the clinic on my shaky ankles I remember how, when he held me upright on the pivot board, the therapist told me to fix my gaze on the wall to find my balance. But I closed my eyes so I could better hear his voice in my ear: *Don't worry. I got you.*

One Last Stand
at the Motel 6

We drive right up to the door. The plastic key tag clatters when you drop it atop the low chest of drawers. The wood is scratched, but not from the grind of hard suitcases. No one ever unpacks here. The TV is bolted to the wall and Gideon's Bible is missing from the nightstand. A Cheez-It crunches beneath my heel when I cross the green carpet.

This time it's Room Eight, which is just like Room Three and Eleven and even the noisy end room, Nineteen, where mold grows in the ice machine just outside the door, yet guests still come to fetch ice cubes because the wind has swept away the hand-scrawled sign *Out of Order*. Eight is good. Eight seems lucky, because I can catch a glimpse of the seaport through the broken venetian blind in the high bathroom window.

The breeze outside is warm and smells of seaweed and damp sand. Yet the motel bathroom is tinged with the odor of Tidy Bowl and wrapped soap. Rust dots the tile and I can practically feel the towels becoming thinner by the minute.

In this, my worst moment—the clinical insertion of my

diaphragm—I can stave off sadness by listening for the waves lapping the shore. I can close my eyes and imagine bluebottle flies buzzing around the stiff spokes of a beach umbrella. Boats glide out of the harbor, their foghorns sounding a mournful blast, and seagulls call.

You sit on the edge of the bed and stub your Camel in the ashtray with the picture of the Charles W. Morgan, Mystic's famous whaling ship, embedded in the thick glass bottom. When I come out of the bathroom naked, you are flopped like a dead fish on the bed, staring at the walls where whale upon whale, uniform as the stitches that once came off my mother's treadle sewing machine, swim around the border of the wallpaper, while underneath in upright Yankee script THAR SHE BLOWS! is solemnly printed and repeated ad infinitum—a proclamation that on our first awkward visit here reduced us to helpless laughter.

Last fall, watching you walk the office halls, I sensed that you, too, did not want a life governed by yellow sticky notes. I imagined you too cringed whenever you heard the ding! of your Outlook calendar calling you to endless meetings catered with muddy Maxwell House coffee and Dunkin' Donut holes brought in by the boss to reward folks for meeting the challenge, making the deadline, being team players. I imagined you too sat in your office idly separating the jumbo from the regular paper clips in your desk drawer and longing for your annual vacation in Florida, where you could shed your shirt and tie and bask in the warm sand.

I knew you felt something for me when you pulled my name in the Secret Santa grab bag and, confined by the ten-dollar spending limit, gave me not a cat calendar nor a fake leather portfolio with a mini-calculator and ballpoint pen, but a brown-and-white striped whelk, which I immediately held to my ear to hear the sound of the ocean.

You wore a wedding ring and so did I. Yet as we sat by the silver-tinseled Christmas tree sipping eggnog and listening to Mel Tormé croak out a carol, you told me a story: in high school you watched a boy drown in the rough waves of Hammonasset Beach following a hurricane. The wooden lifeguard chairs were toppled onto the sand, the grass on the dunes bent back in the wind, and the beach littered with rocks and seaweed and the silver bodies of dead fish, their eyes covered with sandflies. The boy went out on a drunken dare and disappeared into the frothy waves. For a minute, he was nothing but a head bobbing in the churning water, and then he went under. *I watched it happen*, you said. *One of those moments you remember forever*.

Later, in Room Three of the Motel 6, after I grew so full of you I felt like the first Chinese brother who swallowed the sea, you said you sometimes envied the boy, who did not have to grow up and slosh through the slush downtown at Christmastime, looking for a gift for a woman he no longer loved. Lucky boy, who would never grow into a man whose children said, I *know* that, Dad. And when you asked what I might envy about a drowned girl, I said: that she would never have a husband who travels so much he's become nothing more than a voice on the other end of the telephone wire.

If I had you—you said—*I would never leave you.*

This promise seems faded now as the wallpaper, where water bursts only intermittently from the silly little spouts of the THAR SHE BLOWS! whales, reminding me of the swift entrances and exits of the huge, slithering sea mammals I once saw when my parents, so long ago, took me whale-watching in Cape Cod. The boat groaned and tilted and almost tipped, and after whale after whale beat their magnificent slick tails, spraying us with the saltiest water I ever tasted, my mother and father took me to Hyannis, where I sucked on a pistachio salt water taffy and we watched women in Colonial dress dip wicks in the window of a candle shop.

Dead men and women have no regrets. Yet they also have no joyful moments that bob ashore in their memory. These are mine: the time I climbed a lighthouse and looked out over the Long Island Sound, the time I buried a dead seagull with great pomp and circumstance on the no-swimming side of the beach, the time I rode a yellow school bus back from the fifth-grade field trip to Mystic Seaport, clutching my souvenir—a miniature schooner trapped in a tiny bottle with a precious red cork—as my classmates sang, "Four in a bed and the little one said, roll over, roll over!"

Yet this, of all the horrible moments, is the one I'll later recall of you: the distant look in your eyes, as if you were already watching the horizon for the next ship to come in, when I asked, "Do you remember that song about how they all rolled over and one fell out, until there was none left in the bed except the little one who said goodnight?"

Hot Yoga

He comes in late and unfurls his mat too close to mine. During Salutation I hear his every breath. During Noose I see the sweat glisten on his shoulders and rivulet down his bare back. During Triangle he goes left while I go right and we form a half circle. During Corpse we lie side by side with our eyes shut and our minds open and I idly think this is the closest I'll ever come to sleeping with a man who is not my husband.

Then I open my eyes and think: maybe not.

Reason for Return

After Christmas, I unwrapped his presents. The wrapping paper pictured a child in the manger, angels blowing trumpets, and a cornucopia that spilled out in cursive script *Blessings Blessings Blessings*.

I'm known in our house as the thrifty one. I reuse giftwrap from year to year. Collect soap slivers. Turn lotion and shampoo bottles upside down to coax out the last drop. But that day I ripped the angels off each box. Crumpled the *Blessings*. Left the child in the manger in shreds.

Inside the boxes were nestled the kind of gifts teenaged boys love (anything running on a lithium battery) and the mom-kind they merely tolerate (socks, scarves, sweaters, gloves). The last box held a green-and-black buffalo plaid shirt that reminded me of when we had flown cross-country to check out colleges. He had peered out the window at the alternating green and fallow fields below, then said, *Guess I'll miss you and Dad when I'm gone.*

Reason for return? the packing slips asked. They wanted size, color, fit. Since there was no space to write the truth—that you can tell your only child to be careful more times than there are stars in the sky, but you cannot control the carelessness of others—I left the form blank.

I loaded the boxes into the car. What he would have called my *Mothers Against Dunkin' Donuts* ribbon fluttered on the antenna when I slammed the trunk. At the UPS store, a boy around his age stood behind the counter—probably counting the hours, the minutes, until he could clock out and gun his engine home again.

As I set down the tower of boxes, he glanced at the return labels. Yawned. "Looks like nothing worked out."

Love for Sale: 99 cents

Pink foil doilies. Hollow milk chocolate hearts. Spanish-language Valentines.

Red glitter pencils.

I grab a bottle of Ultra Joy.

Get me out of this Dollar Store before I pull a postal on those cheap ceramic cupids.

Car

The only way I can get out of the house is to tell my husband and kids I'm going to the grocery store. But once I get there, I just sit in my car. Just to be by myself. Just to listen to the silence.

It takes everything I've got to go in and face the buttermilk. The string cheese. The flats of stippled chicken wings and five-pound tubs of ground chuck. The blindingly yellow boxes of Cheerios.

Today I sit in my car not only before but after. And while the milk sours and the eggs curdle in the trunk, I remember how the sign in the Toyota dealership read *Let's Go Places*.

Spam

If you don't read this now you will hate yourself forever
Your carpet is an EMBARRASSMENT
Protect yourself from radicals
Find out your credit score with one click
Do you know what your dog's been eating?
MAKE HER SCREAM FOR MORE
Are you going to die?
Cops recommend this!

Phish

Hello, it's me. I know this may sound odd but it happened very fast. I made a trip to Scotland and someone stole my luggage. Inside was my passport and credit cards and all my memories.

Can you please send me some? Preferably the kind that will melt in my mouth like chili-laced dark chocolate. Some should take place in winter, by a fire, with thick snowflakes pelting the windowpane. Others should involve a sturdy man and rumpled bed sheets with shutters that open onto a stormy sea.

My bank said it would take five working days to access the memories from my account, so time is of the essence. I will reimburse you as soon as I return.

Here it is damp and rainy and doctors call me *the lass without a blessed clue who she is*. I want to taste yellow, hear cinnamon, see birdsong, but the nurses just cluck their tongues and murmur, *take a wee sip of this dram, now, yes.*

The Honeymoon is Over

The sign on the side of the road read *furniture, kayak, wedding dress, Saturday 9-12, no early birds.* I sat there gripping the steering wheel, wanting—but not wanting—the light to change.

That night while my husband slept, I crept out to the living room and lay on the couch and watched the moonlight glow on the frayed carpet. Then I closed my eyes and dreamed I was in a wedding gown, paddling in a kayak down a lazy river while overstuffed armchairs and modular sofas and tallboys and lowboys bobbed by. Suddenly I lost my paddle. The water churned white. My heart beat fast as the rapids as the kayak spun toward the cliff.

When I woke, Niagara Falls still pounded in my ears.

I Don't Want Other People to Know Where I Am

Five questions into the quiz and I figure out that FALSE consistently will be the right answer. But the goal is to remain honest with myself, so I keep circling the troublesome TRUEs. *My family and friends would call me stubborn. My co-workers would describe me as moody. I own more things than I need. I am possessive in my personal relationships. I do not take suggestions well. I have trouble controlling my sexual desire. I have difficulty controlling my weight. Sometimes I wish I could run away from home. I have odd sleeping patterns. I often feel inferior to others.*

At the end, the famous author of the famous self-help book asks me to tally the number of TRUEs I've circled. The results are ranked as follows:

1-10: You are in the normal range of the emotional spectrum.

11-19: You are experiencing more than your share of insecurity, anxiety, loneliness, and anger.

20 or greater: You should consult a mental health professional immediately.

I want to pick up the phone and make an appointment. But I keep staring at the statement *I don't want other people to know where I am.* And there—sitting in my car in a deserted parking lot staring at the pigeon shit streaked down my windshield—there, there, I stay.

Swindled

In the family room there's a Keurig coffee maker and a vending machine that dispenses plastic pods of House Blend, French Vanilla, Green Tea, and Dark Chocolate.

DOLLAR BILLS ONLY, it reads.

Over the long course of your illness I feed dollar after dollar into this machine and hunker down on the sagging sofa, nursing my half-hot drink and watching *Beat the Clock* and *You Bet Your Life* and *The Price is Right* and *Let's Make a Deal*.

One day I open my wallet and find only a five. So I take a chance and feed it into the dollar-bill-only slot. When the machine swallows my five but doesn't deliver my French Vanilla, I burst into shameful tears.

You're dying. But all I can think is *I want my money back*.

It Ends the Way
It Always Ends

Tell me why you are here.

    Because my parents sent me here.

    And why did they send you?

    To help me "handle the situation."

    And the situation is. . .

    My brother.

    The *death* of your brother.

    Something like that, I said.

You seem uncomfortable.

    This chair's okay.

    Uncomfortable with me.

    I thought you'd look like my mother.

    Why is that.

    She listens.

    And your father?

    He doesn't want to hear it.

    What does your father want?

For me to man-up.
Which consists of—?
Cracking your knuckles and keeping your mouth shut.
As opposed to—?
Sitting in this chair next to a box of tissues marked PUFFS.

Tell me something about your brother.
    He's dead.
    Something about when he was alive.
    Once we tried to catch a fish. With our bare hands. But it was big and slippery and got away.

How did your brother die.
    Kissed a girl.
    Your brother kissed a girl.
    I just *told* you that.
    Your brother kissed a girl *and*—
    And got meningitis.
    Did you want to kiss that girl, too?
    No, I wanted to grind her so deep into the ground we'd both end up in the grave.
    Grave is an interesting word.
    Grind is even interesting-er.

•

Why didn't you kiss—or grind—the girl?

He got there first.

And you were used to going first?

I was older.

By how much?

I don't know. Eight, nine minutes. How much longer do we have to keep talking?

Why are you so anxious to leave?

Your artwork is ugly.

Why do you say that?

It doesn't have any people in it. Just colors. So you can't figure out what it's supposed to be about.

What do you think life is about?

Being happy. I guess.

Were you happy before your brother died?

Most of the time.

And now?

Everything's fucked.

What did your brother look like?

You know.

I don't know.

You have to know. It's written. Right there. In that file.

Yes, but I'd like to hear it from you. Start like this: *my brother looked like. . .*

Me.

My brother looked like me because. . .

Because he was my—

It's all right.

It's not all right.

There's no law that says boys can't cry. Help yourself to a—

Fucking PUFF.

In your file, it says you're having trouble sleeping. Concentrating. And that the precipitating incident—

What does that mean?

The thing that led you here.

My *parents* made me come here.

—came when your father was trying to teach you how to shave, is that right?

Maybe.

What happened that morning?

Cut myself.

How.

I wasn't looking. The way my dad said I should.

How were you looking, then?

Like... like I wasn't myself. Like I was getting pulled

through the glass, to the other side.

Did you tell your father that?

Sorta.

And what did he say.

Get it together.

Why do you think he said that?

He thinks I'm losing it. I heard him on the phone. I heard him tell you, *I just want my son back*.

Which son do you think he was referring to?

I don't know. My brother. Me. Both of us, I guess.

You don't think he was worried about you? Concerned about your well-being?

You talked to him. So why do you keep asking me this stuff?

I want to know your thoughts. Your perspective. Your feelings.

Why do I have to *feel* something about everything? I don't want to have *feelings*. They don't get you anywhere.

Where would you like to go, if you could go anywhere?

Antarctica. Or someplace so cold you couldn't feel your own feet.

Where would you live?

An igloo.

With who?

Myself, I guess.

What about your parents?

What about them?

Where would they be?

Left behind.

Do you feel left behind?

No.

No because...

Because I don't want to go where my brother went.

What did you feel when you saw your brother in the hospital?

He looked gray. Like a Weimaraner.

And in the coffin?

He looked like an oboe. Or some weird instrument that I don't know how to play.

Did you say anything to him?

It wasn't him.

Did you touch his body?

My mother put a blanket over him. She said she didn't want him to be cold in the grave.

Do you want to tell me something about that blanket?

It was brown. One of the ones she was knitting for us to put on our beds when we went to college.

Did they match?

Everything matched. Except our sides were switched. What I had on the right side, he had on the left.

So when you looked in the mirror you saw both him and you?

Something like that.

You keep looking at the clock.

An hour here isn't really an hour, is it?

Our session is fifty minutes.

So aren't you going to say it?

Say what?

I've seen the movies. It starts the way it always starts: *Tell me why you are here*—and ends the way it always ends—*I'm afraid our time for today is up.*

Yes. Well. I'm afraid our time for today is up.

Mom had dropped me off. But Dad was the one waiting in the parking lot. Staring out the windshield. Like the car was never going anywhere ever again.

He blinked—and looked away—when I got in.

Well? he asked.

I tried to figure out what my father really meant: *Are you cured?* or *Was the shrink worth looking at?*

Mom's prettier, I told him.

Because that seemed man enough.

Research claims

that people who make their beds in the morning are happier than people who don't. So I pull tight the tangled sheets. Smooth the wrinkles on the wedding-ring quilt. Fluff his pillows. Fluff mine.

Research also claims humans shed more than eight pounds of dead skin every year—more during the night than day, and men more freely than women. So I unmake the bed: toss the pillows, rip off the quilt, strip the sheets, pull off the pad, and vacuum every crevice on the mattress.

Then I sit down on what was his side of the bed and wait to molt.

Stroke

My mother and I have nothing to say to one another. And yet she turns to me over the hot stove, eyes beady and sweat balled on her brow. Her head cocks like a chicken about to cluck and out jerk words in a language I do not understand. But I listen closely, because I long to know why it's always been so garbled between us.

Sunday Night & Monday Morning

Sunday night. While my husband's supposedly busting his nuts at the gym, I shave the pills off my cashmere sweaters with his Gillette Fusion.

Monday morning. When the razor slices into his chin, I think, *Your turn to cry now.*

As I See It, Yes

My psychic adviser hung my wet raincoat on the rack. I knew she wasn't a psychiatrist, but I kept waiting for her to ask in a reassuring tone, *What brings you here today?*

Hormones was hardly an intelligent answer. *Love* was even dumber. Still stupider: *the weather.*

I could point to no single reason why superstition suddenly had seized me in its grip. I only knew that last week I had sunk to new lows by asking the Magic 8-Ball if my marriage was going to survive the rainy season and had felt myself grow faint with fear when the answer bobbed up: BETTER NOT TELL YOU NOW.

Then: CANNOT PREDICT AT THIS TIME.

Then: ASK AGAIN LATER.

Warmth

It only costs $249. So even though I live in Florida and it only gets cold enough to use it a few nights out of the year, I order a fake fireplace. The carton announces: *add some warmth to your home without any of the mess or smoke!*

I put the fireplace in the bedroom where my husband's dresser used to stand and remember how he always used to commandeer the thermostat in our house.

Go on Tinder, my friends tell me. Or Match.com.

But it's a lot easier to just flick a switch and spark a flame.

Plus I control the temperature.

Like That

Doctor's appointments. Ballet recitals. Little League games. Bumper-to-bumper traffic. But it was the first time a boy asked me, *You like it like that?* when I realized so much of my life would be waiting for it to be over.

Also by Rita Ciresi

Mother Rocket
Remind Me Again Why I Married You
Pink Slip
Blue Italian
Sometimes I Dream in Italian
Bring Back My Body to Me

About the Author

Rita Ciresi is author of the novels *Bring Back My Body to Me*, *Pink Slip*, *Blue Italian*, and *Remind Me Again Why I Married You*, and two award-winning story collections, *Sometimes I Dream in Italian* and *Mother Rocket*. She is professor of English at the University of South Florida, a faculty mentor for the Bay Path University MFA program in creative nonfiction, and fiction editor of *2 Bridges Review*.

Acknowledgments

Warm thanks to chapbook judge Robert Venditti, Susan Fallows, Lisa Roney and staff of *The Florida Review,* Ryan Rivas and staff of Burrow Press, and the literary magazines that first published these works:

"Bag Boy," *Creative Loafing.* Finalist for the international *Aesthetica* fiction contest, published in *Aesthetica Creative Writing Annual.* Reprinted at *Vagabond.bg.*

"Precipitation: 50 percent," *Pulse: Voices from the Heart of Medicine*

"Second Wife," *Blue Earth Review*

"Physical Therapy," *Hobart*

"One Last Stand at the Motel 6," *AMP*

"Hot Yoga," *Fiction Southeast*

"Reason for Return," *Hawai'i Pacific Review*

"Love for Sale" *Minnetonka Review*

"Car," *Cigale Literary Magazine*

"Phish," *Conium Review*

"The Honeymoon Is Over," *Fredericksburg Literary & Art Review*

"I Don't Want Other People to Know Where I Am," *Lightning Key Review*

"Swindled," *The Healing Muse*

"It Ends the Way It Always Ends," *Lunch Ticket*

"Research Claims," *Almost Five Quarterly*

"Stroke," *Fredericksburg Literary & Art Review*

"Sunday Night & Monday Morning," *Hobart*

"Warmth," *Juked*

"As I See It, Yes," *Sudden Stories: The Mammoth Book of Miniscule Fiction*, Mammoth Books, 2003, Dinty Moore, editor

The Florida Review

The Florida Review is the literary journal published twice yearly by the University of Central Florida. Its artistic mission is to publish the best poetry and prose written by the world's most exciting emerging and established writers. The journal has featured fiction, essays, poetry, and interviews with many notable authors, including David Foster Wallace, Margaret Atwood, Lorrie Moore, Stephen Graham Jones, Gerald Vizenor and Denise Duhamel.

For more information about the Jeanne Leiby Award and The Florida Review, please visit floridareview.cah.ucf.edu.

Subscribe

We thrive on the direct support of enthusiastic readers like you. Your generous support has helped Burrow, since our founding in 2010, provide over 1,000 opportunities for writers to publish and share their work.

Burrow publishes four, carefully selected books each year, offered in an annual subscription package for a mere $60 (which is like $5/month, $0.20/day, or 1 night at the bar). Subscribers are recognized by name in the back of our books, and are inducted into our not-so-secret society: the illiterati.

Glance to your right to view our 2018 line-up. Since you've already (presumably) read our first book of 2018, enter code **WIFE25** at checkout to knock 25% off this year's subscriber rate:

BURROWPRESS.COM/SUBSCRIBE

Second Wife
stories by Rita Ciresi
978-1-941681-89-3

Linked fictional snapshots of feminine lust, loss and estrangement by the Flannery O'Connor Award-winning author of *Mother Rocket*.

Clean Time: the True Story of Ronald Reagan Middleton
a novel by Ben Gwin
978-1-941681-70-1

A darkly comic satire of academia, celebrity worship, and recovery memoirs set in a near-future America ravaged by addiction.

Worm Fiddling Nocturne in the Key of a Broken Heart
stories by Kimberly Lojewski
978-1-941681-71-8

Fabulist, folkloric and whimsical stories featuring an itinerant marionette, a camp counselor haunted by her dead best friend, and a juvenile delinquent languishing in a bootcamp run by authoritarian grandmas… to name a few.

Space Heart
a memoir by Linda Buckmaster
978-1-941681-73-2

The story of growing up in 1960s Space-Coast Florida with a heart condition and an alcoholic, NASA engineer father.

the illiterati

Florida isn't known as a bastion of literature. Being one of the few literary publishers in the state, we embrace this misperception with good humor. That's why we refer to our subscribers as "the illiterati," and recognize them each year in our print books and online.

To follow a specific publishing house, just as you might follow a record label, requires a certain level of trust. Trust that you're going to like what we publish, even if our tastes are eclectic and unpredictable. Which they are. And even if our tastes challenge your own. Which they might.

Subscribers support our dual mission of publishing a lasting body of literature and fostering literary community in Florida. If you're an adventurous reader, consider joining our cult—er, cause, and becoming one of us...

One of us! One of us! One of us!

2017-18 illiterati

Emily Dziuban

John Henry Fleming

Nathan Andrew Deuel

Dina Mack

Abigail Craig

Teresa Carmody

Spencer Rhodes

Stephen Cagnina

Letter & Spears

Matthew Lang

David Rego

Rita Sotolongo

Michael Wheaton

Thomas M. Bunting Projects

Michael Cuglietta

Christie Hill

Alison Townsend

Rick Gwin & Peggy Uzmack

Michael Gualandri

Hunter Choate

Nathan and Heather Holic

Rita Ciresi

Lauren Salzman

Drew Hoffmann

Joanna Hoffmann

Dustin Bowersett

Stacey Matrazzo

pete !

H Blaine Strickland

Karen Price

Leslie Salas

Jessica Penza

Randi Brooks

To a Certain Degree

Yana Keyzerman

Erica McCay

A.G. Asendorf

Sarah Taitt

Winston Taitt

Secret Society Goods

Stephanie Rizzo

Patrick Rushin

Stacy Barton

Marcella Benton

2017-18 illiterati

Roberta Alfonso Malone	Kevin Craig
Catherine Carson	Lisa Roney
Lora Waring	Joyce Sharman
Naomi Butterfield	Amy Parker
Nayma Russi	Martha Brenckle
Nathan Holic	Denise Gottshalk
Mary Nesler	Sarah Curley
Dowell Bethea	Jonathan Kosik
Sarah Wildeman	Pat Greene
Ginger Duggan	Susan Frith
Ashley French	Benjamin Noel
Lauren Groff	Matthew Lang
Susan Fallows	David Poissant
Sean Walsh	Erin Hartigan
Liesl Swogger	Isabel Arias
Shawn McKee	Erika Friedlander
Shane Hinton	Amy Sindler
Janna Benge	Kirsten Holz
John Upperco	Dan Reiter
Peter Bacopoulos	Alexander Lenhoff
Mike Cabrera	Rebecca Fortes
Sara Isaac	Giti Khalsa

2017-18 illiterati

Nikki Barnes
Jeremy Bassetti
Mira Tanna
Chuck Dinkins
Stuart Buchanan
Rich Wahl
Tyler Koon
Bob Lipscomb
Craig Ustler
Lauren Zimmerman
Laura Albert
Emily Willix
Danielle Kessinger
Elisabeth Dang
Vicki Nelson
Camile Araujo
Leslie Salas
Cindy Simmons
Lauren Mitchell
Peter Knocke
Lauren Georgia
Susan Lilley

Jeffrey Shuster
Susan Pascalar
Jessica Horton
Jason Katz
Kim Robinson
Delila Smalley
Christine Daniel
Karen Rigsby
Tod Caviness
Terri Ackley
Terry Thaxton
Danita Berg
Karen Roby
Jesse Bradley
JT Taylor
Ben Comer
Grace Fiandaca
Aaron Harriss
Jonathan Miller
Pamela Gilbert
Nylda Dieppa-Aldarondo
Leeann M. Lee
Gerry Wolfson-Grande

MORE FROM BURROW PRESS

We Can't Help It If We're From Florida
ed. Shane Hinton
978-1-941681-87-9

"As hot and wild and dangerous as our beloved (or is it bedeviled?) state, itself."
–Lauren Groff, *Fates & Furies*

"As weird and funny and beautiful and unnerving as you might expect from some of our state's best writers." –Karen Russell, *Swamplandia!*

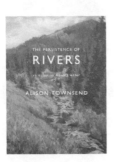

The Persistence of Rivers: an essay on moving water, by Alison Townsend
978-1-941681-83-1

In the vein of Thoreau and Dillard, Townsend considers the impact of rivers at pivotal moments in her life, examining issues of landscape, loss, memory, healing, and the search for home.

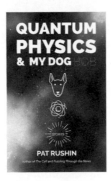

Quantum Physics & My Dog Bob
stories by Pat Rushin
978-1-941681-81-7

Each darkly funny story is like a parallel universe where everyday characters find themselves in a reality slightly askew from the one we know.

The Call: a virtual parable
by Pat Rushin
978-1-941681-90-9

"Pat Rushin is out of his fucking mind. I like that in a writer; that and his daredevil usage of the semi-colon and asterisk make *The Call* unputdownable."
–Terry Gilliam, director of *The Zero Theorem*

Pinkies: stories
by Shane Hinton
978-1-941681-92-3

"If Kafka got it on with Flannery O' Connor, *Pinkies* would be their love child."
– Lidia Yuknavitch, *The Small Backs of Children*

Songs for the Deaf: stories
by John Henry Fleming
978-0-9849538-5-1

"Songs for the Deaf is a joyful, deranged, endlessly surprising book. Fleming's prose is glorious music; his rhythms will get into your bloodstream, and his images will sink into your dreams."
– Karen Russell, *Swamplandia!*

Train Shots: stories
by Vanessa Blakeslee
978-0-9849538-4-4

"*Train Shots* is more than a promising first collection by a formidably talented writer; it is a haunting story collection of the first order."
– John Dufresne, *No Regrets, Coyote*

15 Views of Miami
edited by Jaquira Díaz
978-0-9849538-3-7

A loosely linked literary portrait of the Magic City. Named one of the 7 best books about Miami by the *Miami New Times.*

Forty Martyrs
by Philip F. Deaver
978-1-941681-94-7

"I could hardly stop reading, from first to last."
– Ann Beattie, *The State We're In*